THE MASSEUSE

AN EROTIC ADVENTURE

VICTORIA RUSH

VOLUME 34

JADE'S EROTIC ADVENTURES - BOOK 34

COPYRIGHT

For the uninhibited...

1

Ever since my playdate with Hannah at the rooftop spa in downtown Chicago, I felt a certain void in my love life. I'd enjoyed the various flings with my many lovers over the past few months, but there was always an expectation when the sex was over to move on to the next stage of intimacy. If either partner wasn't ready to invest further in the relationship, inevitably someone's feelings got hurt when one or the other walked away. Every now and then, it was nice to just have a simple, no-strings-attached, take-no-prisoners *hook-up*.

But it was more than that. I longed for the experience of being *feted*, of having my body worshipped by someone whose only focus was giving me the maximum amount of pleasure in the limited amount of time we were together. I wanted to return full-circle to my first experimental foray into the world of anonymous sex at the Fantasy Feast dinner party where I could lie back and let someone service my body. Even if I had to pay for it.

One lonely night when I needed to feel the touch of someone's else's hands on my body, I flipped open my laptop and typed in the search words *private masseuse*. I knew it had to be a female, not a man. Beyond my rapidly increasing proclivity toward having sex only with other women, the kind of massage I had in mind involved more than just the typical therapeutic rub-down. When things got hot and heavy, I needed my partner to keep his dick in his pants while focusing his attention only on pleasing me.

Which was something I'd found very few men capable of doing.

The first few results that came up on the screen provided a list of 'licensed massage therapists' who were available to make house calls in my area. But I knew this was code for the traditional, non-sexual type of massage. Besides, I wasn't sure I wanted my new paramour to know where I lived. Beyond the prying eyes of my nosy neighbors, I didn't want to experience another awkward moment when I had to kick another putative lover out of my house. I wanted to walk in, an *out*, freely on my own terms from this professional relationship.

I scrolled a little further down the page and hesitated when I saw a listing titled *White Orchid Massage–experience the pleasure of tantric massage.*

Okay, I thought. This sounds a little bit more like what I'm looking for. The word 'tantric' suggested a slightly *different* kind of massage treatment.

I clicked on the link and a description appeared beside a picture of a scantily clad masseuse massaging a woman's bare lower back:

Tantric massage is the art of caressing one's body where the boundaries disappear and the recipient learns to experience an elevated and prolonged form of pleasure and relaxation. Your energy flow is stimulated by our personal Goddesses while your senses are gradually awakened toward their maximum potential. Particular attention is focused on attending to the sensitive personal areas of a man's lingam or a woman's yoni. Book a session today to experience the ultimate expression of personal body worship.

Yes, I thought. *That's what I'm talking about: personal body worship. This is what I've been looking for. But who exactly are these goddesses, and what do they mean by a man's lingam and a woman's yoni?*

I clicked on the button below marked *Lingam Massage,* and some black and white illustrations of a woman's hands massaging a man's erect penis appeared with a text box to the side.

The Sanskrit word for the male sex organ is Lingam, which is loosely translated as the 'Wand of Light'. In tantra, the Lingam is honored as the vessel that channels a man's creative energy and pleasure. The goal of the one-hour lingam massage is to caress the entire sensitive area including the testicles, perineum, and the Sacred Spot (prostate), allowing the man to surrender to a new, enlightened form of pleasure. Orgasm is not necessarily the goal, but it can be a welcome and pleasant side effect.

Orgasm isn't the goal? What the hell else do you expect the recipient to experience after one hour of massaging his dick, balls, and perineum?

But I liked the symbolism behind the words 'honoring' his sexual organ and enabling him to experience an 'enlightened form of pleasure'. Something told me that although orgasm wasn't the primary goal, most clients of this special form of massage therapy left with a very happy ending.

But it wasn't *male* pleasure and orgasm that I was interested in. I wanted these special massage goddesses to focus on administering a unique form of female-oriented pleasure. I clicked on the next button marked *Yoni Massage*, and some more erotic illustrations of a woman's hands massaging a woman's vulva appeared with another line of text below.

Yoni is the Sanskrit word for the vagina, which means the 'sacred temple' of a woman's body. During the yoni massage, the Goddess creates a unique space for the receiver to relax, from which she can enter a heightened state of arousal and ultimate pleasure. When orgasm does occur, it is often more expanded and more satisfying. While delivering a yoni massage, the giver should not expect anything in return, but simply allow the receiver to enjoy the experience and lose herself in the prolonged pleasure of being worshipped for the sexual person she is.

Fuck yes, I panted out loud. That's exactly what I wanted. Someone to focus her attention entirely on my pleasure, who'd tease and torment me until I experienced the ultimate form of satisfaction. But even though I knew it would be an entirely one-way form of erotic stimulation, I still needed to be able to connect in some way with my partner. What did these so-called Goddesses look like? I wouldn't be able to truly immerse myself in the experience if I didn't find her attractive.

My gaze shifted to the menu on the sidebar, where a map displayed red pins showing the location of White Orchid goddesses in major cities throughout the United States. I clicked on the pin centered over Chicago and a photo of a pretty African-American girl named Violet appeared with a link for more details. The page opened with a picture of a dark, slender woman about my age wearing a skimpy leotard that hugged every inch of her lithe figure. It showed her leaning over a massage table while caressing the upper thighs of another woman lying face down with a small towel barely covering her upturned ass.

But it was *Violet's* ass that drew my immediate attention. Slender and curvy with separate volleyball-sized globes, the downward seam of her tights divided them into perfectly shaped spheres that made it look like her butt had been carved out of marble. I felt my panties begin to dampen as I imagined watching her sylphlike figure flexing and bending while she laid her hands on my body. I read the brief bio beside her picture, then my attention was drawn to the top of the page where a drop-down menu outlined her list of services.

I clicked on the Yoni Massage button, where some erotic pictures of Georgia O'Keefe floral artwork framed the detailed description of her ninety-minute intimate massage sessions. Although the verbiage referred to cryptic terms such as 'somatic pelvic floor exercises' and 'sexual energy cultivation techniques', I had little doubt, just as with the thinly-veiled symbolism of the Georgia O'Keefe paintings, where exactly she intended to focus her attention.

The massage sessions were provided at her personal studio and offered in blocks of four, each lasting roughly ninety minutes, with home assignments and email check-ins between sessions. There was no appointment form or payment link–only an email address where I was encouraged to leave a detailed message with my personal details and booking requests. I immediately clicked on the link and began composing a carefully worded message:

Violet,

I'm interested in booking a session for your one-on-one personal yoni massage. I work from home, so I'm available pretty much any time to meet at your studio, but weekends are my preferred time to concentrate on personal enrichment.

Please let me know the next available slot you have to fit me in. I look forward to learning more about your tantric exercises and experiencing your enlightened form of body worship.

Sincerely,

Jade

After I clicked send, I immediately winced at my not-so-subtle choice of words asking for a 'slot' to fit me in. But as I continued scanning her website page further describing the yoni massage procedure accompanied with more illustrations of the masseuse probing her client's orifices in various sexy positions, I pulled down my panties and thrust my fingers inside my hole, mimicking the Goddess's techniques.

You can press your fingers into my slot any way you like, I panted, running my eyes over her tight figure while I hunched over my keyboard feeling my pleasure beginning to rise...

By the time I finished coming down from my self-induced orgasm, I already had a new message notification in my in-box. I opened my mail and excitedly clicked on the message from GoddessViolet.

Jade,

Thank you for your inquiry regarding my services. I have an opening for yoni massage this Sunday at 2 p.m. if that works for you.

My fees are $600 for a four-massage package, with each massage offering a deeper and more intense stimulation of your sacred temple. I also offer a separate introductory massage for $200.

Please click on the PayPal link below to select and make advance payment for your preferred option. Once you complete the payment, I'll send another email with the address for my studio.

I look forward to our time together and feel blessed to share these transformative practices with you.

Love and blessings,

Violet

After reading her message, I sat back in my chair, contemplating my options. Six hundred bucks was a considerable sum, and although everything looked above-board on her website, I still couldn't be sure this wasn't some kind of scam. I clicked on the payment link and chose the two hundred dollar introductory option, then waited patiently for a reply with the additional details. It took a painfully long time for her to reply, but after she confirmed receipt of my payment and provided me with the location of her private studio, I breathed a sigh of relief.

For the next three days, I grew increasingly excited about my upcoming encounter, shaving my legs and armpits twice to make sure there'd be no unnecessary friction between any part of my skin and Violet's soft hands. Fortunately, my earlier laser hair treatment had already removed the last traces of any hairs from my mound and vulva. I must have come at least ten more times lying in front of my dressing room mirror imagining the sexy masseuse exploring every inch of my body.

By the time Sunday came around, my skin already felt like pins and needles in anticipation of Violet's tantric caresses. There was something about the idea of lying down and letting somebody bring me to the height of pleasure while she watched me writhe and moan in front of her that drove me crazy with desire. I'd always enjoyed having someone manually manipulate me to orgasm as much as oral or full-contact sex, knowing they could just sit back and savor my sexual response while concentrating all their energies on pleasing me.

When I drove to the address provided by Violet in her email, I was relieved to see it wasn't a cheap strip mall typical of those quick rub-and-tug operations. On the contrary, it was a beautiful luxury highrise with a commanding view of Lake Michigan only a few blocks away. If this was her primary source of income, I thought with a smile, she must run a pretty good book of business. I parked my car in the guest parking area then headed to the foyer where I buzzed the button for suite 2402.

"Hello?" a soft voice answered after a brief pause.

"It's Jade," I said. "I have a two p.m. appointment."

There was a loud buzz and I opened the unlocked entrance door then made my way to the elevator bank. I found it odd that she hadn't offered a more friendly greeting before buzzing me in, and during the long elevator ride to the twenty-fourth floor, I suddenly began to have second thoughts.

Just how safe is it to be walking into a stranger's highrise on the pretense of anonymous sex? I'd always wondered why most masseuses preferred to provide the service at their clients' homes rather than their own residence. Was this some kind of trap where someone just *pretending* to be Violet enticed me into his home only to hold me prisoner and have his way with me?

I was just about to tap out a warning message to my best friend Hannah on my phone when the elevator opened. The hallway was tastefully decorated with plush wool carpets, brightly illuminated wall sconces, and expensive brass door fixtures. I peered down the corridor in the direction of Violet's apartment near the end and put my phone back in my purse.

Fuck it, I said to myself, shaking the cobwebs out of my head. *If someone wanted to lure me into some kind of dangerous arrangement, they wouldn't do it in a place like this. Or give me their address, which I could easily share with my friends. She's probably doing this at her place as much to protect herself as me.*

When I reached her door, I paused to summon my courage, then tapped twice on the shiny lacquer surface.

Even the entrance to her 'studio' is upscale and enticing, I thought.

When the door swung open and I saw Violet peering out at me with a sweet smile, I breathed a sigh of relief. She was wearing a long silk kimono with a single white orchid nestled in the side of her upswept hair held back in a pretty bun. She was lighter-skinned than she appeared on the website, and with her smooth, caramel-colored complexion, large brown eyes and full sensuous lips, she reminded me of young Beyoncé.

"Good afternoon," she said standing to the side, motioning for me to enter her apartment.

When I walked through the door, she offered to take my coat then hung it in the adjacent closet. She led me to a large living room dominated by floor-to-ceiling windows displaying an unobstructed view of Lake Michigan, glistening like a sparkling jewel in the mid-afternoon sun. Her apartment was tastefully decorated in a minimal Japanese ethos, with a low-slung sectional sofa, large glass coffee table, and floral prints of George O'Keefe paintings on the wall. In the center of the room stood a long massage table covered in a white terrycloth towel.

My pussy fluttered at the sensual imagery of the setting and I peered at Violet with raised eyebrows.

"Wow," I said. "I've never had a massage in such a beautiful place. You have magnificent taste in your decor."

"Thank you," she said, motioning to a closed door a few feet behind her. "If you'd like to get changed, you can use my powder room. You'll find a cotton robe hanging on the back of the door."

"Thank you," I said, taking her cue to not waste any time and opening the door to the change room.

When I got inside, I closed it softly behind me, then leaned back against the partition while staring at myself in the oval mirror over the vanity.

Holy fuck! I mouthed the words silently, looking at myself in disbelief. Not only was Violet even more beautiful in person than she appeared on her website, her massage studio was something out of a fantasy dream. This wasn't some cheap massage parlor where you'd walk in for a quickie then hightail it out of there so as not to be seen. This was more like the luxury upscale spa Hannah and I'd gone to a few months earlier where we were feted and spoiled for much of the day. The difference was that in *this* place, I had both the masseuse *and* the exquisite surroundings all to myself for the next ninety minutes.

As I began disrobing and neatly folding my clothes on the tasteful sidestand to the left side of the sink, I began singing the melody to the Beyoncé song Irreplaceable.

To the left, to the left
To the left, to the left
Everything you own in the box to the left
In the closet that's my stuff, yes
If I bought it please don't touch...

I'd always thought the singer was one of the most beautiful women I'd ever seen. I must have watched the sexy video of that song a hundred times, fantasizing that it was me squatting over her sexy legs while she sat in front of her makeup mirror in a slinky negligee. And now I had the chance to relive my fantasy with a dead ringer who was about to touch me in the most intimate way.

After I removed all my clothes, I looked at myself in the mirror appraising my naked, freshly primped body. I still had a pretty sexy figure for a woman in her mid-thirties, with firm plump breasts sitting high on my chest, a narrow, toned waist, and long slender legs. I wondered how much attention the *front* of my body would get from Violet during this first encounter. I knew most masseuses only attended to the back of their clients' bodies while focusing on relaxing and removing the knots from their muscles, rather than stimulating the more erogenous areas of their figures.

No matter, I said to myself, slipping my arms through the sleeves of the waffle-patterned robe hanging on the back of the door and tying the belt loosely around my waist before swinging the door open.

Either way, I planned to give my sexy masseuse ample access to my 'sacred places', whether I was lying face down or face up.

3

―――――

When I emerged from the powder room, I was surprised to see that Violet had removed her robe and was preparing her tools on a side table next to the massage table. Instead of the long silk robe, she was now wearing a thin cotton tank top with matching white cotton tights. The tight fabric clung to every curvature of her body and when she swung around to greet me, I gasped audibly when I saw her full figure for the first time.

Her breasts were petite, but they had an exquisite elongated, scooped shape that made the front of her skimpy t-shirt tent and bulge with prominent sensuous darts poking out from her hardened nipples. Her thin cotton tights also left a minimal amount to the imagination, as the soft fabric flowed over her flat pelvis and sensuously curved hips to her shapely, well-toned legs. I could see the cleft from the slit of her pussy as the fabric clung to her like a second skin, daring me to soak up her body with my wide eyes. In a way, it was even *more* erotic to see her cloaked in the soft white covering barely concealing her dark areolas and sexy camel toe, beckoning for me to approach her closer.

"May I take your robe?" she said, holding out her Madonna-toned arms in front of her.

"Um–yes," I stammered, momentarily pulled out of my trance.

I turned around and she softly pulled the robe off my shoulders then placed it on a side table beside the sofa. I peered at the massage table inquisitively, then turned back around to face Violet.

"Do you want me to lie face up or down?" I said, unsure of the protocol with this new procedure.

"Let's go face down to start," she smiled, extending her arm toward the table.

I lifted my right knee and climbed onto the bench, extending my legs straight down behind me. There was no customary hole at the head of the table where I'd normally place my face to relax my neck muscles, so I turned my head to peer out over the wide expanse of sparkling blue water. As soon as I saw the soothing picture of the gently lapping waves and reflected sunshine, I immediately began to feel the sexual tension ebb away. Whether this was by design or incidental, I wasn't sure. But for a few brief moments, I forgot about the primary purpose for my visit and flitted my eyelids in sublime bliss. Even if I just had to lie here watching this spectacular scenery for an hour and a half, it would almost be worth the two hundred dollar price of admission.

But it didn't take long for my *other* senses to be awakened as Violet opened her scented bottles of massage oil and the smell of jasmine and chamomile filled my nostrils. I breathed the heavenly scent in as I expanded my lungs and my chest rose and fell gently on the padded table. I could hear the sound of oil dribbling into her hands as she turned one of the bottles upside-down, then rubbed them together slowly. My pussy quivered knowing that she would soon lay her moistened hands on my skin, and I extended my arms to my side, inviting her to begin touching me.

I was a little disappointed when she started at the foot of the table with my feet, but I smiled peering up at the large analog clock hanging on the near wall, knowing she had a full ninety minutes to explore the rest of my body. I relaxed the muscles tensing in my shoulders and buttocks, happy to bide my time while she worked her way up toward my waiting temple.

As she separated each of my toes between her slippery fingers and kneaded them softly and sensuously, I was tempted to talk to her to break the awkward silence. But I knew from previous massages that masseuses preferred to work in silence, encouraging their clients to relax and let all the external distractions melt away. The whole point of a massage was to concentrate on the soothing feeling of being caressed, and I had no intention of disrupting Violet's mojo at the outset of our erotic encounter.

But that didn't stop me from letting my mind wander to all manner of sexual imagery while she squeezed and kneaded my extremities. As she pulled her fingers slowly down each of my toes from the ball of my foot to the toenails, I imagined it was my *clit* she was pinching between her fingers while she stroked my hard shaft and teased the tip of my nub. Whenever she slipped her fingers between my toes, I channeled her inserting her slender digits between my dripping *labia*, feeling my wet tunnel gripping her tightly. And when she grabbed my feet and pressed her thumbs against my soles while she pulled my toes against her washboard-hard tummy, I imagined toe-fucking her pussy while she gripped me in the throes of passion.

By the time her fingers moved to my ankles and began

working their way up the inside of my calves, I was already soaking wet while I unconsciously ground my mound into the moistening towel beneath me. I spread my legs apart, inviting Violet to move closer to my apex, but she seemed in no hurry to attend to my quivering pussy. Instead, she wrapped her fingers around the curvature of my calves, rubbing them softly and slowly with her warm, slippery hands. Unlike the firm and sometimes painful kneading of my muscles that most masseurs were accustomed to administering, her touch was always light and sensuous, focused instead on titillating and stimulating every square inch of my skin. Reflecting back on what I'd read on the White Orchid website, I knew that she had a plan for eventually reaching my 'sacred temple', with the goal of heightening my arousal to achieve the 'ultimate pleasure'.

I tried to relax my arms and the rest of my body while she worked her way further up the inside of my thighs, but I couldn't help curling my upturned fingers in a come-hither motion in the direction of my aching sex. But just as her thumbs began probing the edges of my tumescent lips, she suddenly shifted position and moved up to the *head* of the table, placing her moist hands on my shoulders and upper back. This time I could detect the scent of my own juices intermingled with the aromatic massage oil as her hands slid over my pliant skin, and I turned my head away from the direction of the lake to watch Violet more closely.

As she stood to the side of the long table to gain better access to my upper back, I stared at her crotch while she leaned and stroked my shoulders and neck softly. The fabric of the white cotton tights pulled and stretched as she swayed her body overtop of me, and I could feel my mouth beginning to water while I imagined sucking her sweet pussy into my mouth. She must have known what was on my mind while she did this, because she hesitated for the longest time pressing the bottom of her undergarments sensuously against the padded corner of the table while she moved her hands progressively further down my back.

I was disappointed when she shifted position once again, denying me ready viewing access to her lower body, but I smiled when I noticed a small wet spot forming in the seam of her pants below her vulva. This time, she moved her hips directly over the top of my head while she extended her arms further down the center of my back toward my flexing buttocks. She placed her thumbs together, sliding them sensuously down the valley in the center of my back, and I lifted my ass, trying to narrow the distance between her probing fingers and my puckering lips. Making my torment all the more intense, while she pressed her palms further down my back in a series of forward-and-back movements, she gently pushed her pubis against the back of my head.

Whether she was doing this for her own amusement or mine, I couldn't be sure. But it took every ounce of my willpower not to lift my head and clamp onto her pussy like a wild boar catching its prey after a long chase through the underbrush. By now I was panting heavily, and she must have felt my breath on her upper thighs straddling either side of my head. As she neared the small of my back with her probing thumbs, I tilted my hips as far as I could in her direction, pointing the cleft of my ass directly up toward her face. The further she probed down my body, the closer her torso leaned over the surface of my back, until I could feel her pointy breasts and hard nipples touching my skin.

I groaned quietly, begging her to press her fingers into my crack. When she finally did, my cheeks quivered, antici-pating her reaching my aching sex. Instead, she wrapped her hands around the globes of my ass and squeezed them firmly, tantalizing me with the tips of her fingers as they touched the outside edges of my external labia. I grunted more loudly and swiveled my butt in circles, signaling to her that I was desperate for her to administer to my yoni as her website had promised.

Recognizing my impatience, Violet released the pressure on my buttocks and threaded her thumbs into my crevasse, rolling them softly over my puckering rosebud. I groaned like a cat in heat when I felt her touch my sensitive tissue, and I spread my legs further apart to make it easier for her to slide her fingers over my crescent toward my swollen lips and buzzing clit. As she leaned her torso more firmly atop my back and pressed her mound harder against my moistening head, she began angling her palms inward, caressing the outside of my dripping labia with the tips of her fingers while she continued stimulating my sphincter with her thumbs. The combined sensation of her fingers probing my anus and the edges of my widening gash simultaneously was driving me crazy with passion, but she still hadn't touched me in the most sensitive area that would lead me toward a much-needed orgasm.

When she finally began pressing her fingers further down my crease toward my flaring slit and pinching my folds between her index and middle finger, sliding them sensuously along the length of my engorged labia, I hummed a sigh of pleasure knowing it wouldn't be long before Violet finally brought me to sexual nirvana. But just as she began pressing her digits into my pulsing hole, I heard a soft chime and she withdrew her hands from my private areas as quickly as she had entered.

I twisted my head to peer up at her inquisitively, and she turned around to face the large clock on the wall while reaching over to the side table to dry off her dripping hands with a small towel. I looked up at the clock and was horrified to see the large hand pointing straight down, marking the completion of our session at three-thirty. Somehow, in all the heat of the slow buildup, I'd completely lost track of time.

"It appears that our time's up for today," Violet said nonchalantly. "I hope you enjoyed your introduction to tantric massage."

So that's her game, I thought, shaking my head in dismay. *She suckers me in with this so-called introductory session, driving me to the point of near-delirium then sends me packing just as I'm about to get off. Talk about a honey trap.*

I was pissed beyond belief, but the sight of Violet standing before me with the front of her cotton ensemble drenched in a combination of massage oil and my own sensual juices soon made me forget about her questionable business practice. The wetness had made her t-shirt nearly transparent, and I gawked like a newborn baby at her large brown medallions and pointed nipples pressing against the thin fabric. Even the front of her *tights* was soaking wet, pulled up between her flaring labia at the base of her mound. I wasn't sure if it was from her own juices released while she was grinding against my head or from the sweat pouring out of my hair as I got increasingly turned on, but it didn't matter. All I could think about was continuing her program of tantric massage and getting as close as I could to this beautiful goddess again as soon as possible. She had me hooked like a fish, and she knew it.

"How soon are you available for another session?" I asked meekly, sitting up on top of the giant wet spot I'd created in the middle of the massage table.

4

<hr>

After my equally titillating and frustrating initial massage session with Violet, I had to wait a whole week to see her again. In the intervening time, I vacillated between fuming over the disappointing ending she'd delivered and reliving her slow but intense buildup. Even though I didn't experience my usual climactic finish, I hadn't felt so turned on for so long in a very long time.

During my subsequent masturbation sessions, instead of rushing toward orgasm in the usual manner, I brought myself close to the edge repeatedly, resisting the temptation to fall over the precipice and quickly come down from my highs. There was something strangely liberating about being able to sustain such intense pleasure for as long as I wanted without always feeling the need for the final payoff. If this was what tantric sex was all about, I was rapidly becoming a passionate proponent of the mysterious practice.

By the time the following Sunday rolled around, my entire body was buzzing from my extended edging sessions, and I was eager to feel Violet's magic hands upon me once again. When I arrived at her studio and she opened the door, she was already wearing her sensuous white cotton undergarments, and we wasted no time getting started.

"Face up or face down?" I asked succinctly after shedding my street clothes in her powder room.

"Down," she said, equally matter-of-factly.

I climbed up on the padded massage table and extended my arms behind me, turning my head to peer out at the calming expanse of blue water extending out to the horizon. This time I was determined to relax and simply enjoy the voyage Violet took me on, realizing this process was far more about the journey than the destination.

She began once again at the foot of my body, but this time, instead of clasping both of my feet at the same time, she focused her attention only on my left foot, caressing the hard instep and my soft sole with gentle circular motions of her moistened hands. I could smell the gentle aroma of apple intermingled with the other scented oils, and my mouth began to water once again imagining myself lapping up her juices as she approached my erogenous zones. The combination of her firm kneading of my dorsal bone and the soft pressing of her digits into the pliant flesh of my sole reminded me of the sensation of a lover running her hands down over my pubis into the loose folds of my vulva. I purred like a kitten soaking up the exquisite slowness and eroticism of her touch.

As she shifted toward the top of my foot, instead of moving up the insides of my lower legs, this time she rolled her hands over the bump on the outside of my ankle like a pitcher softening up a baseball before delivering it to the opposing batter. Except in this case, I was transfixed by her pre-delivery ritual, already losing focus on why I was hunched over the plate, watching her graceful movement in the reflection of the big picture window.

When she began running her hands up along the outside edge of my leg, I couldn't help flexing my calves and thighs in autonomic response to her sensuous touch. As she approached my downturned pelvis, she slipped her fingers under my hips, tracing the curved ridge along the top of my crest. Although her fingers never got closer than a few inches from my tingling mound and pussy, the feeling of her sliding her fingers over my hard bone was one of the most erotic sensations I'd ever experienced.

I tilted my body a few inches away from her to give her some more space, and she pushed me further onto my side, with the front of my body now facing her. I turned my face to peer in her direction and was happy to see her newly oil-stained bodysuit displaying her beautiful brown skin underneath.

As she began running her palms over the side indentation of my waist, I could feel the goose bumps on my skin beginning to rise while I watched her tits jiggling in her tight tank-top. Although the upper part of her ensemble wasn't as wet as the lower portion, I could see her large brown areolas and protruding peaks through the light-colored fabric, daring me not to ogle them like a star-struck fangirl.

When she placed her palms on my quivering tummy and began moving her hands toward my mashed-together breasts, my mouth opened unconsciously, desperately wanting to suck on her succulent teats. I could feel my own tips hardening the closer she got to my mounds, and when she encircled them with her palms, rolling the tips between her thumbs and forefingers, I gasped at how delicious it felt. I'd heard rumors how some women unconsciously reached orgasm from breast-feeding their babies, and now I understood how sensitive this part of the body could get when properly stimulated and caressed.

I groaned as Violet cupped my breasts, teasing me ever-so-gently with her warm, oily hands and soft fingertips. I probably could have come if she'd continued twisting and rolling my nubs for much longer, but just as before, she moved on just as I was nearing the turning point. I was sad to see her take her attention away from my engorged tits, but what she did next soon had me wishing she'd climb on top of me and have done with me.

Tilting my upper body further back, she pressed her palms firmly against my upper chest while she spread her fingers apart approaching my neck. As she encircled my narrow isthmus, I tilted my head up, and she squeezed my throat gently with the open palms of her hands. I'd never felt so vulnerable and sexually charged having someone else's hands on me, and I grunted like a wild animal lost in the clutches of a predator. While she was doing this, I could have sworn that her nipples pressed even further out against the flimsy fabric of her cotton t-shirt, and I detected a slight upward curl of her lips as she grasped me in the delicate embrace.

Was she getting just as turned on as I was from all this sexy imagery?

If so, I was more than happy for her to take whatever further advantage she desired of me, feeling my body's sexual energy rapidly rounding second base. But she obviously had no intention of suffocating me, and her hands continued their upward momentum as they rolled over my chin and jawline. When her apple-scented fingers moved next to my lips, I opened my mouth and she curled them into my cavity while I sucked on the tasty juices and kneaded her phalanges playfully with the tips of my teeth.

Two can play this game, I smiled, preventing her fingers from pulling out of me while I glared up at her with piercing eyes.

Instead of trying to remove her trapped fingers from my mouth, she curled her thumbs around the dripping edges of my lips, tracing a line around the raised edges, mimicking the caress of my outer labia. When I unconsciously groaned from the symbolism of her erotic touch, she pulled her fingers out from my loosened grip, then glided them up the side of my cheeks toward the bottom of my ears, curling them around their perimeter and pinching her fingers around the outside edges.

By now, I was moaning like a cat in heat and twisting my body in sexual abandon, eager for her to take me anyway she could. Her slow, teasing buildup was driving me crazy with desire, and I clasped the sides of her forearms, trying to pull her toward me. But she tensed the muscles in her strong arms as she resisted my attempt, running her oily fingers through my hair and over the back of my scalp. I didn't care for a millisecond that she was making a mess of my carefully coiffed hair while I looked up at her, begging her to fuck me.

Seeming to acknowledge my torment, she pulled her hands away from my face and moved them slowly across the side of my shoulder, tracing a line down the side of my arm with the lightest of touches, making my hairs stand up on end. When she reached my hand, she interlaced her fingers with mine, then lifted my arm, pressing it over my head. Then she clasped the underside of my upturned limb, threading her other hand with equal tenderness up the soft skin on the other side. When she reached my armpit, she paused for a moment, massaging the indented space firmly with her oily thumbs, now even further moistened from the saliva of my mouth.

"Oh God," I moaned, amazed at how her touching me in every place other than the most sensitive areas of my body could make me feel this electrified.

With my arm still held gently over the top of my head and lying pinned on my side, my breasts were pulled off-center and rolling atop one another, creating a new kind of sensation I hadn't felt before as my oiled flesh rubbed sensuously together. All the time I was moaning with every hair on my body standing on end, Violet watched me with her big doe eyes and glistening lips. I wanted desperately for her to lean over and suck my bullets into her mouth, bringing me to orgasm just like the breastfeeding mothers I'd heard about, but I knew that was too much to hope for at this still-early juncture.

She angled my arm gently back down onto my side, placing it softly on the table in front of me, then traced a line all the way down the hourglass-shaped side of my back, up and over the curvature of my ass and down the back of my upper thigh, pausing to caress the tender space behind the back of my knee. Then she pronated her hand and pulled my knee slowly up toward my hips, forcing my legs into a bent-knee scissor position.

I was now lying on my side on the massage table, drenched in massage oil, with my legs splayed into a side-split position, with the glistening gash of my billowy cunt freely displayed for her viewing pleasure. I could feel my juices pouring out of me while her gaze turned toward my slit, dripping over my engorged lips and down the front of my lower thigh. I felt incredibly sexy and exposed in this compromising position, and if she'd so much as *blown* anywhere in the direction of my flaring snatch, I'm sure I would have come in a nanosecond.

Realizing I was now about as aroused as I was ever going to be, Violet slowly rolled her palm over the arc of my upturned hip and turned her hand sideways, curving the side of it softly between the crack of my ass. The feeling of her oily hand slicing my cleft like a soft bread knife was another sensation I'd never felt before, and I tilted my pelvis toward her, desperately trying to bring her hand closer to my aching clit.

Clearly trying to extend my agony as long as possible, she waved the side of her hand gently up and down the length of my crease, stimulating my anus and the lower reaches of my opening with a slow, measured touch. Growing increasingly impatient, I glanced up at the wall and noticed that it was three-fifteen. There was only fifteen minutes left for Violet to bring me to the peak of pleasure. I was all for the idea of extending this intense feeling as long as possible, but sometimes a girl just needed to get off.

Noticing me peering up at the clock, Violet opened her hand and pressed her fingers further down toward my slit. When she reached my opening, I was elated when she curled them inside me, pressing her three middle fingers deep inside my tunnel. I groaned in excitement, angling my hips to extend them as far inside me as possible. For a few brief moments, I was content to simply hump her fingers embedded inside me, but the angle of her hand reaching over from the side made it difficult for her to stimulate my G-spot in the usual manner.

I twisted my hips in a circular motion trying to angle her hand in the direction of my most sensitive part and we she realized what I was attempting to do, she began flexing her index finger forward and back, finally caressing the magic spot on the inside of my pussy. I groaned in delight at the pleasant sensation, but something was still missing. As much as I was enjoying the feeling of her fingering my hole and teasing my G-spot, I still needed some direct contact with my clit.

I tilted my hips further upward, sliding her pinky up the outside edge of my labia and when I felt it make contact with my tingling gland, I groaned deeply, finally beginning to feel the familiar pangs of my orgasm approaching. Seeking to add more pleasure to my rapidly building excitement, Violet simultaneously extended her thumb toward my tight pucker as she circled her pinky over my swollen bulb.

Fuck yes, I thought, growling like a wildcat. Finally, she's hitting all the right buttons. I could feel my orgasm rapidly approaching, and I gripped the sides of the massage table while I stared at Violet's sexy tits pressing against the soft fabric of her t-shirt, preparing for the inevitable release. But just before I passed the moment of no return, the dreaded chime sounded again, and Violet paused with her hand deeply embedded in my tunnel. For a brief moment, I thought she was going to continue to finish me off, and I groaned when she began to pull her hand out of me.

What the fuck? I thought, panting wildly. *This isn't tantric massage—it's tantric torture! How can she do this to me, knowing how much I needed the ultimate release her website had clearly alluded to?* As she slowly began to clean up, I couldn't help asking the obvious question.

"That was wonderful," I said, sitting up reluctantly. "But when are you going to take me to that magical place of enlightenment your website promised?"

"Remember, the purpose of tantric massage isn't just about reaching sexual climax," she said, wiping the oil nonchalantly from her hands. "It's an opportunity for you to connect with your inner feelings and extend the pleasurable sensations to their maximum degree."

"But your website suggested that when orgasm is achieved this way, it is often more expanded and intense than usual. Isn't that one of the sensations you help your clients achieve at some point in this process?"

"Yes," she said. "But remember, you still have two more sessions in your scheduled package. Most of the pleasure is experienced during the slow and extended build-up."

"Okay," I said. "But I don't know if I'm going to be able to hold out much longer. What can I look forward to during my next session?"

"At stage three, the process will become more interactive, with closer contact between the two of us, adding an extra level of stimulation and excitement. I think you'll find the next stage in your journey takes you to an entirely new level of fulfilment."

I wasn't entirely sure what she meant by more *interactive*, but if it involved more body contact with her magnificent figure, I knew that would be more than enough to allow me to achieve my ultimate goal.

"You're a very demanding coach," I smiled. "I'm looking forward to improving my batting average the next time around."

"Next time we'll see if we can deliver some *home runs*," she nodded, adding to my athletic analogy.

5

———

I had to wait another week to see Violet again, and in the intervening time I came many times reliving the exhilarating experience of her caressing my most sensitive regions. At the last session she'd finally gotten around to touching my clit, but she'd left me hanging at the edge of another powerful orgasm. I was beginning to grow tired of this tantric 'edging' technique. After all the teasing and intense build-up, I was shaking so much by the time she finished that I could barely walk out of her apartment and back to my car.

At my next session I was determined to get off even if I had to grab hold of her and mash my pussy into her face until I climaxed. She'd promised that this massage would be more interactive, and as I drove to her apartment, my mind raced with all manner of exciting visions. Would she finally suck my throbbing pearl into her pretty mouth? Was she going to mount me and grind her sexy body against mine? Was it too much to hope for her to take off her skimpy leotard and let me see her glorious naked figure unencumbered for the first time?

By the time I got to her building, my panties were already soaked through imagining all the different ways we could interact in the ninety minutes we had together. But when she opened the door to her apartment, I was disappointed to see her clad once again in her cotton tights. I'd hoped we could jump-start this process of interactive discovery by being able to touch her in the way she'd been touching me. I'd spent long hours dreaming about how I could tease and drive her crazy with desire before finishing the two of us off in a climactic crescendo.

This time, I didn't even bother putting on the robe on the back of the change room door. Instead, I pranced out into the middle of her living room stark naked, not wanting to waste a precious second getting started.

"Face up?" I said, glancing at the massage table standing in the middle of her room framed by her floor-to-ceiling windows and the beautiful expanse of Lake Michigan extending for miles into the horizon.

"Down," she said matter-of-factly.

No worries, I thought, taking my time to give her an unobstructed view of my glistening snatch as I lifted my knee to climb up onto the table. *If this massage is anything like the last one, there'll still be plenty of chances for her to access my private parts.*

As I lay down on the padded table, I turned my head in the direction of the lake and closed my eyes with a contented smile. There was something incredibly exciting about the idea of lying naked on a platform designed for no other purpose than caressing another person's body and waiting to see exactly where and how my paramour intended to arouse me. As I listened to Violet preparing her materials on the side table next to my stand, my entire body tingled in preparation for her erotic touch.

But this time, the first thing I felt touch my body wasn't her fingers. It was a warm flat stone, placed between my shoulder blades, just below the nape of my neck. While it was a pleasant sensation, I was disappointed to find her resorting to traditional massage techniques. I was eager for her to get on with the erotic aspect of the massage, mindful of how quickly our previously scheduled time had slipped away from us.

But as she began to place successive hot stones down the ridge of my spine in the direction of my butt, I could feel my pulse quickening. Each stone seemed warmer than the one before, and by the time she reached the small of my back, my buttocks were quivering imagining what she planned to do next. The stones were hot enough to make my skin burn momentarily, but soft and gentle enough to send a shiver down my spine.

Violet paused for a moment, knowing my mind was racing with what she intended to do with the stones. When I felt her place the next one on its side and begin sliding it toward the crack of my ass, I tilted my pelvis toward her. She drew the edge of the rock into the top of my slit, then pulled it back toward the base of my spine, making me squirm in anticipation.

The idea of her caressing my underside with these exotic stones was something I'd never even considered. Unlike my cold, plastic- or silicone-covered sex toys, this massage aid was definitely new and unique. Of course, the fact that there was an incredibly sexy person on the other end of them teasing and caressing me *also* elevated the experience beyond my usual self-administered masturbatory sessions.

As Violet continued to tease me by sliding the edge of the oiled stone in and out of the top of my crease, I moaned and flexed my buttocks in a vain attempt to clamp the object and encourage her to move it further down in the direction of my pussy. When she finally slid it over my quivering rosebud, I squealed at the sublime sensation of the warm, slippery rock against my sensitive skin.

I'd never been particularly excited about anal sex, but the feeling of this sexy goddess probing my most private area with this smooth oblong object was something new altogether. The shape of oil-covered stone seemed perfectly designed to slide through my fissure, now thoroughly greased and ready for whatever she had in mind. I resolved there and then to add these erotic rocks to my repertoire of sex toys and experiment with them at home as often as I could.

When Violet began sliding the stone lower toward the base of my slit, I could feel the oil dripping down and over my folds, causing me to groan more loudly. I spread my legs apart, encouraging her to go lower, and when she dipped the smooth edge of the stone into my slit, I grunted, pressing my mound hard against the table. As she began to sensuously probe the outer edge of my pussy with the object, I rocked my hips in tandem with her movement, feeling the pleasure beginning to rise within my body.

She pressed the stone further into my gap, and for a moment I thought she was going to release it and let it float inside me like some kind of oversize, heated Ben-Wa ball. As much as that might have increased my pleasure by placing it closer to my G-spot, she seemed determined to maintain control and continue torturing me while I humped the massage table ever more frantically.

But once again, just as I was approaching the peak of my pleasure, she withdrew the stone from my hole and placed it flat against my opening. I glanced in the reflection of her living room window and saw her peering at my dripping pussy and quivering ass, then she looked up, smiling back at my reflection.

"Time to turn over," she said softly.

In the three sessions we'd spent together so far, we'd barely strung three or four complete sentences together. But somehow, this strong, silent treatment only added to the excitement of lying helplessly in her hands.

"My pleasure," I said, flipping over like a fish out of water at the knowledge that she'd finally have direct, unfettered access to my aching clit.

But instead of moving the stone further up my channel toward my buzzing gland, she reached over to her side table for a new stone, dipping it in a bowl of hot oil. When I felt it dripping on my bare mound and stomach as she lifted it over the surface of my body, I gasped at how delicious it felt. While I stared up at her with pleading eyes, she took the edge of the searing stone and began tracing it softly around the edges of my areolas.

I peered down the front of my body and saw my nipples standing firmer than I'd ever seen them before. Whether this was from my skin recoiling at the sensation of the hot stone touching it or from the heightened sense of arousal I was feeling seeing Violet watching me as my body responded to her touch, I wasn't sure. But either way, I was in heaven as I tilted my head back and raised my chest up toward her angelic face. I closed my eyes, hoping this was just a prelude to her finally climbing up on the massage table with me, as she'd alluded to her final comments at our last session.

But for now at least, she seemed content on teasing me by sliding the side of the stone around the perimeter of my areolas, then softly over the tips of my tingling teats until I was writhing uncontrollably on the massage table. Recognizing how turned on this was making me, she alternated between teasing my nipples with the edge of the stone and laying it flat against the surface of my breasts while rolling it softly over my soft and pliant flesh.

While she was tormenting me with this erotic dance of warm stone caresses between my breasts, I noticed Violet grinding the base of her mound against the side of the massage table next to me. It took every ounce of my willpower not to reach up and pull her down on top of me where I could properly fuck her. But I was prepared to give her a little longer, knowing that she'd promised to deliver a 'home run' after our last session together. I still wanted to feel her build me up to the height of pleasure, then allow me to release my pent-up excitement in one final, gigantic orgasm while she watching me writhing and moaning inches before her eyes.

After stimulating my nipples and breasts for a few minutes, she finally began rolling the stone down the front of my quivering stomach toward my aching pussy. I smiled at the inventive ways she used the device to tease me, with the rolling wheel adding to the imagery of her steering toward my final destination. But when she got to my bare mound, instead of rolling the stone further down toward my tingling clit, she paused over my hard pubis, flattening it so I could feel its full radiant heat on my trembling pelvis.

As she swiped the warm pebble closer and closer to the base of my mound and my buzzing clit, I lifted my hips higher and higher off the surface of the massage table. Desperately wanting her to place the rock over my tingling gland, I glanced up at the clock, wondering if she was going to leave me hanging once again on the edge of release.

When she noticed me looking up at the clock and seeing

we only had ten minutes remaining in our session, she suddenly grasped my ankles, pulling my body down the massage table toward her as she spread my legs apart. I looked up at her in surprise, and she smiled back at me while she calmly replaced the lukewarm stone with two hotter black stones. Then she placed each one on the inside of my ankles, slowly sliding them up the inside of my calves and thighs.

While she did this, I spread my legs even further apart, giving her an eagle-eye view of my gaping vulva. It must have been a tantalizing sight with her face only inches away from my splayed pussy, dripping down the sides of my thighs and ass cheeks in a virtual cascade. As I twisted and turned my hips, begging her to touch my cunny directly with the rocks to put me out of my misery, she turned them once again onto their sides and pressed them hard against the outside edges of my labia while she slid them forward and back along my opening.

With each rhythmic movement, she pressed the stones closer and closer together, until they were sandwiched between the palms of her hands. As I lay before her in my prostrated position with my legs splayed and my knees bent, she began rolling and pressing the stones deeper into my slit. When I felt them approach the top of my folds and touch my clit, I gasped, lifting my hips even higher above the table.

As the joined tablets rolled over my nub and along the sides of my erect shaft, Violet eased up on the pressure. The hollow created between the two rounded stones acted as a perfect conduit for my engorged gland, and she smiled while she teased my clit with gentle forward and back rocking motions. With my hips now pitching and rolling in escalating need, she finally separated the stones and placed one of them flat atop my burning jewel. At first, she just held it there for a moment while I reveled in the exquisite feeling of the smooth, hot rock radiating its energy into my core.

But when she began to turn the rock in a slow twisting motion against my glans, I whinnied in pleasure at the unique feeling of the warm object pressing against my aperture. As I began to feel my pleasure beginning to rise like an oncoming tidal wave, Violet slid the other rock vertically into my tunnel, rolling the edge of it against the inside front surface of my pussy on my G-spot. The combination of the sustained brushing of the warm stone on my burning bean and the gentle rolling of the stone over the underside of my clit soon brought me once again to the brink of pleasure.

As I peered down toward Violet, I noticed the front of her tights were now soaked with a large wet spot while she ground the base of her pussy against the corner of the massage table. Seeing her enjoying herself almost as much as me while she watched me grunting and groaning under her ministrations soon took me over the edge. As I felt my orgasm begin to consume my body in one cataclysmic earthquake, I gripped the side of the massage table with both hands, and jetted my pent-up juices all over Violet's pretty tank-top while I stared at her pointy tits as she slumped over the base of the table in a simultaneous climax with me.

I must have remained in this epileptic state for a minute or longer, because by the time I finally came down from my intense climax, my entire body was quivering in exhaustion. When I peered back up at Violet, she was still hunched over the end of the massage table, breathing heavily in her own post-orgasmic bliss. This wasn't exactly what I envisioned by her cryptic comment at the end of our last massage session when she suggested the next two sessions would be more 'interactive', but I smiled knowing I still had one more appointment remaining in my scheduled package.

As I peered back up at the clock realizing our time had finally run out, my mind was already racing ahead to my next chance to touch this gorgeous African-American goddess flesh-to-flesh.

6

———

Thankfully, I only had to wait three more days for my next appointment with Violet. Whether this was because she was just as excited as me to explore the next step in our rapidly escalating engagement, I wasn't sure. But one thing was certain. This last session was going to be 'interactive' in the fullest sense of the word, whether she intended it or not. After we'd shared a brief moment of mutual intimacy, there was no way I was going to let her off the hook with another one-way massage encounter. I'd fulfilled my goal of lying passive while she brought me to the height of passion manually. Now it was time for us to merge our bodies together and experience a whole *new* kind of tantric pleasure.

I could barely sleep during the intervening nights as I lay awake planning all the different ways we could stimulate each other and achieve the penultimate pleasure her website had alluded to. Although the first three sessions had been exciting with each one increasing my degree of arousal, there were still plenty of ways I could think of to ramp up the action and give both of us an opportunity to reach our maximum potential. I'd read somewhere that most people took less than eight minutes to complete the act of sexual congress. An hour and a half of dedicated erotic touching was more than enough time for each of us to enjoy an incredible build-up and an earth-shaking climax. And I had every intention of giving Violet just as good as I got.

When I arrived at her apartment at the scheduled time, we went through the usual preliminaries, with me lying dutifully facedown on her terrycloth-covered massage table. But this time, instead of pouring the massage oil into her hands and proceeding to rub me down like the previous times, she tipped the bottle of warm liquid over my ankles and drizzled it in two long, sensuous streams up the back of my legs, curving over the arch of my buttocks and leaving a small puddle in the small of my back.

This was new, I thought, feeling the liquid slowly spreading over my ass cheeks as it flowed into my crack and dribbled down my cleft onto my puckering lips and tingling clit. *But why so much—and why only on my legs?*

When she placed the palms of her hands on my ankles and began to slide them up the back of my legs, spreading the oil evenly over my calves and thighs, I wasn't sure what she was up to. But when I heard the table suddenly creak and the bottom of the cushion indenting from a heavy weight, I squirmed my hips in delight. She was finally getting up on the massage table where we could press our bodies together and experience a different kind of body contact!

As she spread my feet apart, I felt her kneel between my ankles, then she placed her palms on my skin, pressing them firmly into my flesh while her thumbs teased and tickled the inside of my legs. When she reached the top of my thighs, her oily fingers circled tantalizingly at the edge of my opening, then she spread my cheeks wide apart while she squeezed my globes. I could feel my pucker being stretched and twisted while she did this, and I wondered just how much she was enjoying seeing me spread apart for her viewing pleasure.

I shimmied my ass, encouraging her to touch me more closely, then she slid her thumbs over my rosebud, rubbing it sensuously in little concentric circles. When I squeezed my buttocks, grinding my mound into the padded table, she pressed my legs together and straddled the back of my thighs with her knees. I could feel her mound pressing against the back of my ass, and I tilted it up, encouraging her to hump me while she stimulated herself.

She raised her hands off my butt, and I heard the sound of clothing rustling behind me. When I peered in the reflection of the glass and saw her pulling off her tank-top, I tilted my head, struggling to peer at naked torso. I'd waited almost three weeks to see her undressed, and I didn't want to miss one precious second of soaking up her gorgeous body. But she leaned forward, pressing my shoulder blades back down onto the cushion, then she dipped her tits into the warm puddle of oil still resting in the small of my back. When I felt her hard nipples on my skin, I groaned, trying vainly to reach around my sides to caress her beautiful ass. But she seemed to have other plans, sweeping my hands to the side and forcing my arms back to the side of my body. Then she arched her spine, pressing her mounds into my flesh as she slowly crawled over my ass.

Feeling her whole body touching mine for the first time

was sublime, and I squirmed and mewed while she body-fucked me with her writhing figure. When her head reached my shoulders, I could feel her cool breath on the back of my neck, and I turned my face in the other direction, hoping to meet her lips. But she continued sliding up my body as her tits separated over my nape, where I saw her dark areolas and long nipples tantalizing me beside my cheek. I flapped my mouth open like a fish lunging for a lure, but she kept her berries just out of my reach.

I could feel the heat of her body against mine and the aroma of her exotic scent commingled with the massage oils, and when she moved slightly higher pinning my waist to the table under her hips, she rubbed her oily breasts over the back of my head. I thrashed my head wildly from side to side, not minding for a second that she was making another mess of my freshly washed hair. When she leaned over and rested her elbows on the pad beside my ears, I could feel her wet crotch humping the small of my back, soaking up the rest the oil in the cotton cloth of her tights. *God*, how I wanted to flip over and see her pretty cunny revealed in the drenched, thin fabric!

I could hear Violet's breathing beginning to escalate and become raspy as she ground her pussy into my back, and I curled my fingers up to the sides of her thighs, caressing her with my hands. Recognizing that I was ready for some more direct engagement, she sat up and angled her knee against the side of my hip, signaling for me to turn over. With both of us now thoroughly coated in oil, I shifted my body and slowly flipped over, lingering for a moment at the sensation of my hips pressing into her gap while sliding over her dripping crotch.

Two can play this game of tantric teasing, I thought, smiling up at her.

But when I saw her magnificent tits for the first time with her large brown nipples, I lost any semblance of self-control, straining to lift my body to bring my face closer toward her. She smiled back at me and leaned forward to meet my face, and I sucked her teats hungrily into my mouth, engulfing them like a hungry calf feeding on her mother's udder. The oil had a pleasant citrus flavor, and I hummed happily that she'd been thoughtful enough to use edible oil, wondering if this was standard practice or if she'd simply taken my cues that I was ready for a different kind of engagement.

But with my face buried in her bosom and my hands squeezing her exquisite melons, it hardly mattered. For the next few minutes at least, I had her all to myself, and I was finally free to do as I pleased. Knowing that our time was soon going to run out, I reached down with my hands and pulled her ass higher up on my chest until she was straddling my face. When I saw the outline of her pussy through the transparent fabric of her tights, I tilted my head and began to suck on the wet cloth. But it was difficult for me to get traction on her clit with the barrier between us, even as she pressed her hips harder into my face while I nibbled on her the best I could with my teeth and stretched lips.

It felt glorious to be licking her pussy finally, but I was impatient to taste her directly and plunge my tongue into her dripping tunnel. Violet glanced up at the clock over the head of the table, then she lifted her legs and turned her body around, tilting her ass invitingly toward my head. When I saw her cotton-clad butt resting inches away from my face, I threaded my fingers under the waistband of her tights and began to pull them down over her hips. They bunched up near the top of her thighs, and she raised her hips over my head inviting me to pull them down all the way, and I practically ripped them off her body, throwing them onto the floor beneath us.

It looks like both of us will have some cleaning up to do after this, I smiled, staring at her glorious, naked butt for the first time.

Her skin was a beautiful chocolate brown color, but the folds of her vulva were bright pink, glistening with a mixture of scented oil and her own juices. I pulled her ass down hard onto my face and began gnawing on her like a wild animal with a bone. As much as I'd dreamt about slowly teasing and tormenting her the way she'd done with me, when I finally had the chance to ravish her, I couldn't resist the temptation to dive in head first.

When my lips encircled her pearl and my tongue slid over her nub, she pressed her pussy down harder onto my face, moaning softly. Exhilarated to finally have the chance to return the pleasure she'd given me, I began circling my hips unconsciously, and Violet lowered her head onto my own pussy, taking me into her mouth as we sucked on each other's clits, mashing our oily tits against one another's abdomens. The feeling of our warm bodies sliding over our joined skin was electric, and it didn't take long for the combination of erotic sensations to begin triggering the feeling of an oncoming climax.

But as our twisting and moaning began to escalate in pitch and volume, and I could feel myself nearing the point of no return, Violet suddenly lifted her head off my pussy and shifted her hips forward, away from my face. I tried to keep her from moving further away, but her heavily oiled skin didn't provide any traction, and she straightened her body up as she lifted her knees over my shoulders, sitting down over my chest. Desperate not to lose touch with her, I reached up with my hands, caressing the sides of her breasts while I rolled her nipples between my fingers.

She let me have my way with her for a few more seconds as she rolled her wet pussy all over my chest and tits, fucking each one of my breasts while she slid my rock-hard nipples between her dripping slit. Noticing my hips dry-humping the air over the massage table, she slowly inched her hips down the front of my stomach until she was straddling my bare mound. As she began to rock her hips over my hard pubis, she leaned forward, revealing her pretty bronze starfish for the first time.

Unable to resist the sight of it flexing and winking at me as she ground her cunt into my mound, I reached down with one hand and ran my thumb over her in the same way she'd done with me earlier. The sound of her grunting and moaning indicated that she was enjoying being touched there just as much as I did, and I was about to slip a finger in her hole when she pulled her body down a few inches lower, tantalizingly out of reach.

But when I felt the soft flesh of her folds at the base of her pubis meet my own, I tilted my hips forward and let out a long, guttural groan. The feeling of our pussies meeting for the first time was heavenly, and I strained to rock my hips under her weight in an effort to rub our clits together. But it was difficult for us to position our pussies in such a way for each of us to get the necessary friction we both desired, so Violet spread my knees further apart, kneeling on the padded table between me. Then she lifted my knees and pulled my legs back until I was in an upside-down squatted position.

With my dripping crease now perfectly positioned for her grinding pleasure, she spread her knees apart and crouched overtop of me, then lowered her pink vulva directly onto mine. When I felt her warm flesh melding against my own, I squealed in pleasure, flapping my hips against her. I felt a bit embarrassed humping her so impatiently, but I was mindful of the clock ticking behind us, and there was no way I was going to let her end this session without both of us achieving the height of pleasure.

Fortunately, she seemed just as committed to reaching climax before our time ended, and as the two of us slapped our bodies together moaning with increasing pleasure, I tilted my head up, watching her beautiful ass bobbing up and down over my gaping slit. The sound and smell and feel of her magnificent body writhing against my own was a combination of sensations I couldn't resist any longer. As our moaning escalated toward our inevitable denouement, I turned my head toward the window and saw Violet peering back at me with her head tilted back in ecstasy and her mouth mawing open at the brink of ecstasy.

When our orgasms finally pounded over the two of us, we watched each other pitching and whining in mutual climax with the sparkling reflection of Lake Michigan shining upon us in supernatural splendor. When our orgasms finally began to subside after what seemed like an eternity, Violet leaned forward resting her torso on the base of the massage table between my legs while I peered down watching the juices dribbling out of her pretty flower onto our connected mounds.

I glanced up at the clock over my head and smiled, noticing that we'd gone a full fifteen minutes over our allotted time. Something told me this final session in my allotted massage package wouldn't be the last time the two of us had a chance to explore a transcendent level of enlightened pleasure.

Ready for more erotic chills and thrills? Check out the entire collection of full-length stories in Jade's Erotic Adventures in your favorite store:

Click to view your favourites...